ROARY®

The Racing Car

Roary and Friends

Ton-Up Tunnel

Dinkie's Corner

Shank Chicane

Tight Turn

Quickturn Corner

Starting Grid

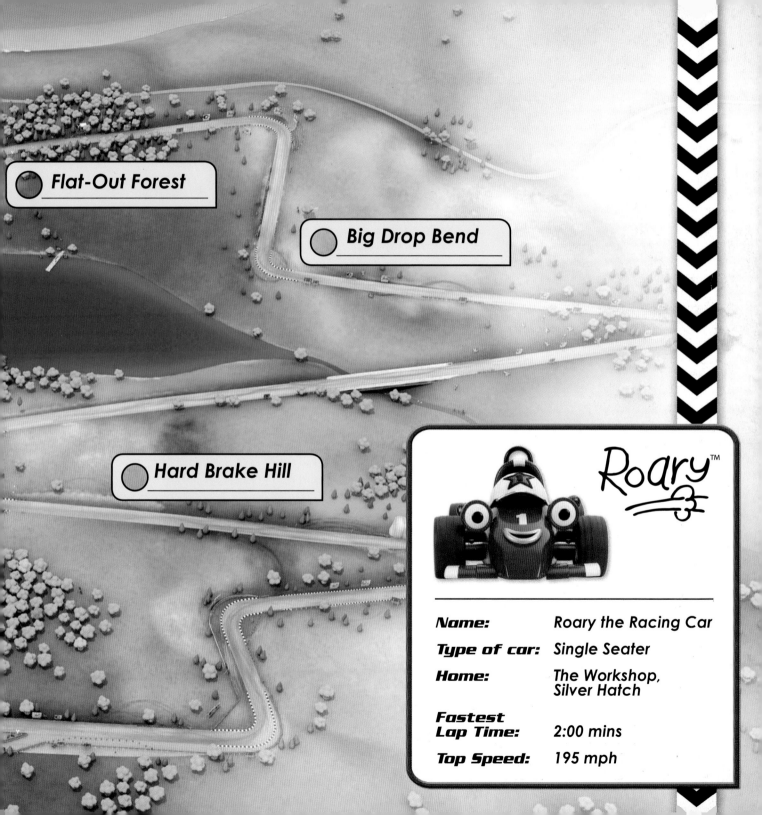

Flat-Out Forest

Big Drop Bend

Hard Brake Hill

Roary™

Name:	Roary the Racing Car
Type of car:	Single Seater
Home:	The Workshop, Silver Hatch
Fastest Lap Time:	2:00 mins
Top Speed:	195 mph

1 2 3 4 5 Let's GO!

First published in Great Britain by HarperCollins Children's Books in 2009

1 3 5 7 9 10 8 6 4 2
ISBN: 978-0-00-731602-1
© Chapman Entertainment Limited & David Jenkins 2009

Visit Roary at www.roarytheracingcar.com

Text by Mandy Archer

Printed and bound in China

Roary

HarperCollins *Children's Books*

Vroom, vroom!

Watch Roary zoom into pole position!

Roary is the newest racing car at Silver Hatch racetrack. He's a single seater with a shiny red bonnet and a powerful engine. Roary wears a white cap with a bold number one printed in a star on the front.

Roary has a need for speed. The lively little car loves zooming down straights, screeching round corners and leaping extra-fast over Tummy Turn Bridge.

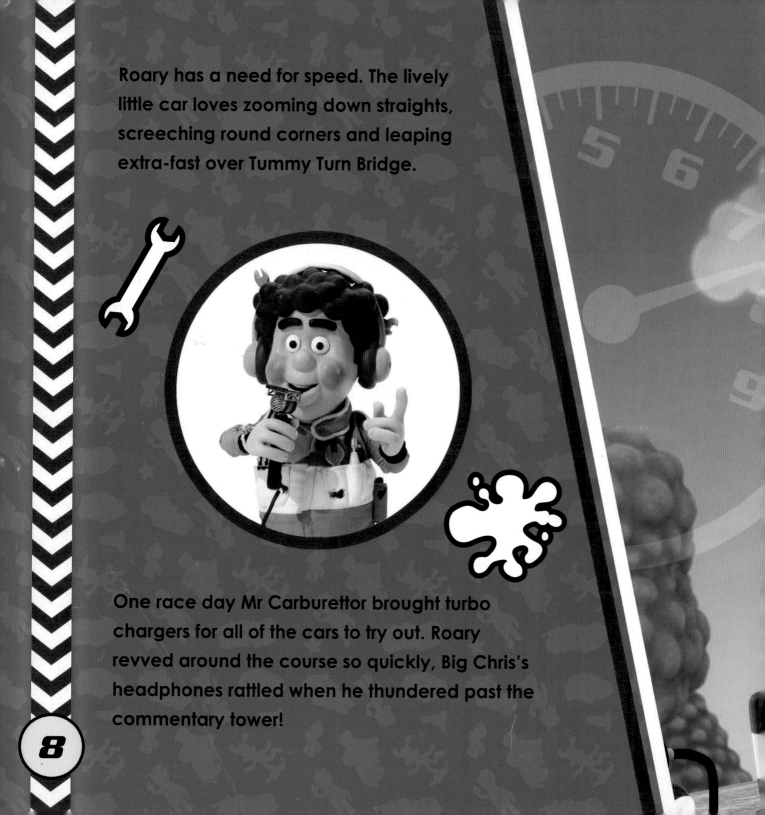

One race day Mr Carburettor brought turbo chargers for all of the cars to try out. Roary revved around the course so quickly, Big Chris's headphones rattled when he thundered past the commentary tower!

Roary lives in the Silver Hatch workshop with the rest of Mr Carburettor's racing team. He has the number one parking spot, right next to Maxi.

The workshop is fitted out with everything that Roary and his friends need to stay on the road. There's a special ramp for oil changes, a cable that pumps air into their tyres, plus spanners and wrenches in all shapes and sizes.

On Roary's first day at Silver Hatch, Cici took him for some practice laps around the track. He didn't think he'd be able to keep up with Maxi and the others, but Cici showed Roary that anyone can win if they really try!

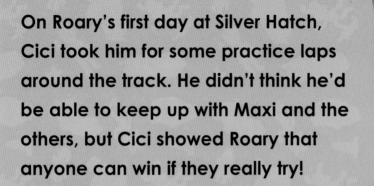

Cici's daring driving and crazy stunts always make Roary gasp. When the little pink car challenges him to a race, Roary pushes his pistons and gets set for some super fast fun!

Catch me if you can!

Roary's friend Big Chris runs the workshop at Silver Hatch. Even though he can be a bit forgetful at times, Roary thinks that he's the best mechanic in the whole world.

When Roary feels sad, Big Chris cheers him up by singing songs or tickling his spark plugs. At night-time he sits down to tell bedtime stories. Roary loves it when Big Chris calls him his number one star.

If you bend it, you mend it!

Roary and Big Chris share all sorts of high speed adventures!

Once when Big Chris was fixing Flash's skateboard, he couldn't resist having a go himself. The poor mechanic zoomed out of control, sending Roary screeching to the rescue. Big Chris managed to jump off the board and grab Roary's bonnet just in the nick of time.

Maxi is Roary's racetrack rival.
The Italian Formula One champion
boasts that he's the fastest car in
all of Silver Hatch.

Mamma Mia!

Roary can't help but rumble his engine when
he hears Maxi demanding superstar treatment.
Mr Carburettor makes sure his favourite gets the
best of everything, from expensive new tyres to
top grade fuel.

When Maxi gets too big for his bumpers, Roary motors away to play with FB. FB is a friendly 1950s truck who works for Farmer Green.

FB wishes that he could burn rubber like the Silver Hatch gang, but flat bed trucks aren't built to race! When FB helped Roary fetch milk and eggs for Big Chris, his friend arranged for the truck to do a special lap of honour around the racetrack.

Slow and steady can win the race!

Often, on their day off, Roary and his pals skid down to Silver Hatch Beach. One afternoon Big Chris was so impressed with the sandcastle that the cars had made, he topped it off with Marsha's green starter flag!

Roary's friends do so many things to make him smile. His favourite Silver Hatch surprise was a birthday cake with icing and a big blue candle!

Roary loves to push past the speed limit, but he's still got lots to learn about racetrack rules. The cheeky car can't help hurtling headlong into all sorts of trouble.

Even roaring red racing cars need to slow down sometimes! One morning he and Cici were zooming so fast around Harepin Bend, Roary span off and landed in a puddle of thick, squelchy mud!

It's not always easy being the youngest racing car on the grid. Sometimes the single seater can't resist revving up his engine, even when it's time to pull into the pit lane.

One afternoon Roary tried to help Big Chris by minding the workshop. When Maxi cruised in for an oil change, Roary decided that he and Flash could do the job all by themselves. They made a big mess and it took the team hours to scrub the oil off the garage floor!

No matter what the result is on race day, Roary will always be a winner in Big Chris's eyes.

Silver Hatch wouldn't be the same without the little red car wheel-spinning round the workshop. Even Mr Carburettor agrees that Roary is the team's very own number one star!

Light 'em up! ⭐1

ROARY
The Racing Car
○ Roary and Friends ○

Roary

Big Chris

Rusty

Flash

Drifter

Plugger

Mr Carburettor

Hellie

PC Pete

Nick

James

Marsha **Zippee** **Maxi** **Cici** **Tin Top**

Molecom **Dinkie** **Farmer Green** **Flat Bed**

Breeze **Loada** **Big Christine** **Mama Mia**

ROARY
The Racing Car

Roary and Friends

Collect
the set!

Other books in the range

Roary and friends

Roary

Roary and friends

Big Chris

Roary and friends

Maxi